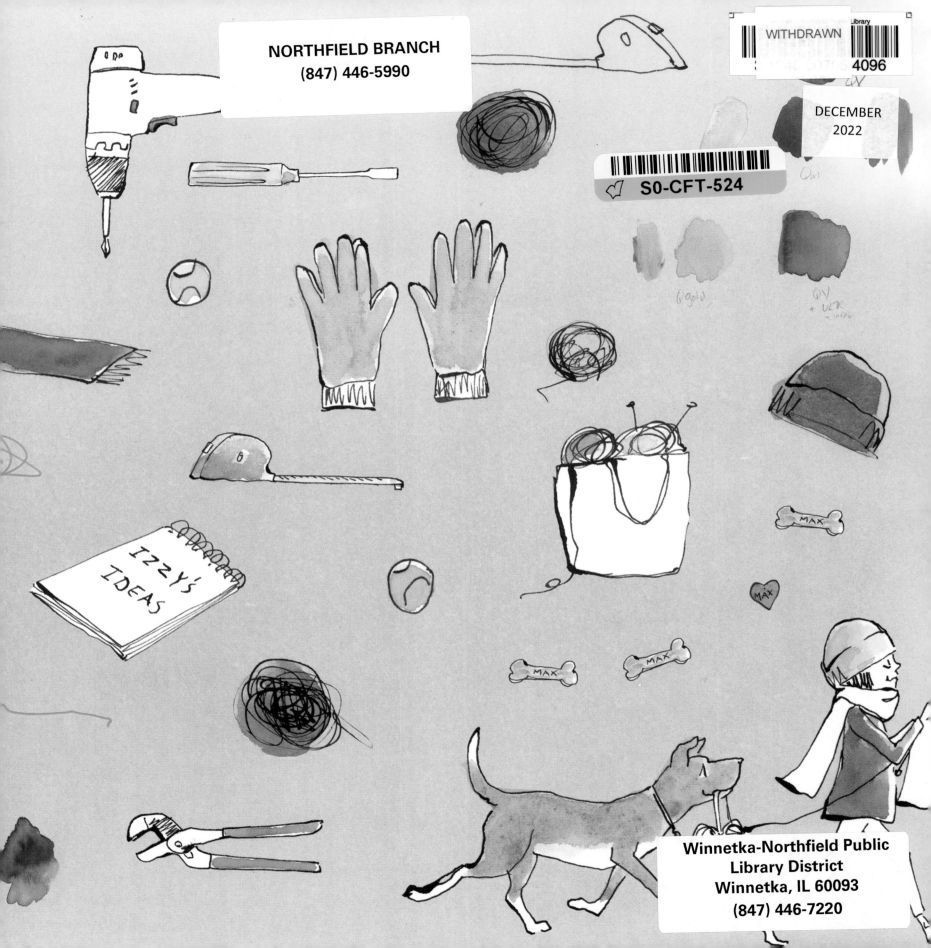

With much love to Big Peter, Jack, Rich,
Wendy, Dave, Carolina, Peter, Jessie, Becky, Kenji
and James, Lucas, Lizzie, Hazel, Helen, Julián, and June

Copyright © 2022 by Laurel Molk

All rights reserved. Published in the United States by Random House Studio,
an imprint of Random House Children's Books, a division of Penguin Random House LLC, New York.

Random House Studio and the colophon are trademarks of Penguin Random House LLC.

Visit us on the Web! rhcbooks.com

Educators and librarians, for a variety of teaching tools, visit us at RHTeachersLibrarians.com

Library of Congress Cataloging-in-Publication Data is available upon request.
ISBN 978-0-593-43458-1 (trade)—ISBN 978-0-593-43459-8 (lib. bdg.)—ISBN 978-0-593-43460-4 (ebook)

The text of this book is set in 16.5-point Baskerville.

The illustrations were rendered in watercolor, pen-and-ink, and a sprinkling of Photoshop.

Book design by Rachael Cole

MANUFACTURED IN CHINA

10 9 8 7 6 5 4 3 2 1

First Edition

knitting
for dogs

Laurel Molk

RANDOM HOUSE STUDIO

NEW YORK

Max is a big dog who lives with Izzy,
a medium-sized girl with big ideas.

Izzy loves making things,
all kinds of things.

Birdhouses, bee houses, a wooden swing . . .

. . . a tent for two,

and even a catapult for Max.

So when Izzy took up knitting, she thought it would be easy.

And it was.

She knit stripes, checks, and hearts.
A long scarf, a warm hat.

Then Izzy started knitting herself a sweater. But it wasn't quite right.

Izzy turned it this way and that, but she couldn't figure out how to fix it.

"Max," explained Izzy, "sometimes it's best to just start over again."

So this is what she did.

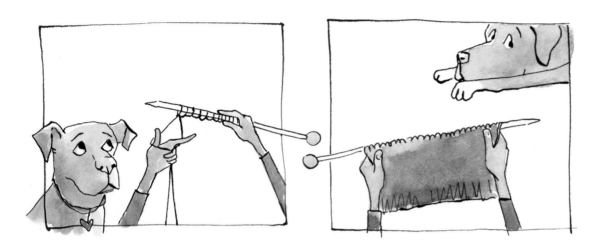 

The second sweater was
no better than the first.

"Max," explained Izzy, "failure is part of the creative process. We just aren't used to it."

Izzy gathered yarn and knit a third sweater. But it was another
knitting disaster. Each sweater was worse than the one before.

So many mistakes, too large, too small, too loose, too tight,
sleeves that simply weren't right.

"Max, Max, what should I do?"

Knitting wasn't so easy after all.

Izzy could make birdhouses, bee houses,
a swing, a tent, and even a catapult.

Why couldn't she make a sweater that fit?

Max made a warm, cozy nest with the cast-off sweaters.

Izzy sighed. "At least they're good for something, Max."

And then Izzy came up with an idea.

A **GREAT** idea.

A new and wonderful idea.

Grabbing her scissors, Izzy shouted, "Max, you're a genius!"

And with a couple of snips here and a few stitches there, Izzy

changed a sweater full of mistakes into something **FABULOUS!**

"It's not at all what I planned," she told Max.

"But I think it's even better! Much better, in fact."

"Arf! Arf!" approved Max.

Warm as toast, Max raced to the park with Izzy.

While all the other dogs played, a skinny little dog
huddled under Max, shivering.

Izzy knew just what to do.

She and Max dashed home,

and came back with another fabulous sweater remake.

Soon everyone at the park
was bringing Izzy yarn.

She knit up a storm, with Max by her side.

Once upon a time there was a spotty dog named Max, who along with his fearless friend Izzy saved a dangerous dragon from a surfeit of chocolate-covered cherries.

Before long, **ALL** the dogs at the park were wearing Izzy's creations.

By now, Izzy was sure she could make herself

a sweater that fit. But that was not the case.

Izzy turned it this way and that.

"No worries, Max," she said.

And with a couple of snips here
and a few stitches there . . .

Izzy took the sweater that didn't work and made it into something wonderful.

"It's not quite what I intended," said Izzy, "but in some ways, it's even better. Much better, in fact."

Max agreed.

Easy Scarf

If you want to try knitting, here's a beginner's project. You can ask a knitter to show you how to cast on, work in garter stitch, and bind off. You can also find knitting lessons online.

You will need:

3 balls of bulky/chunky yarn (more if you want to make a longer scarf)

Knitting needles size US 13

Gauge: 9 stitches = 4 inches

Cast on 15 stitches.

Work in garter stitch (knit all stitches in a row).